Santa's Snowball Fight!

Santa's Snowball Fight!

Written and Illustrated by Sue Ann Alton Sanders

Photography by Santa Paul H. Behrens. ORDM

Santa's Snowball Fight!

Written and Illustrated by Sue Ann Alton Sanders

Photographed by Santa Paul H. Behrens, ORDM

Copyright © 2023 by Sue Ann Alton Sanders

Charleston, SC
www.PalmettoPublishing.com

First Edition

Hardcover ISBN: 979-8-8229-2160-3
Paperback ISBN: 979-8-8229-2161-0
eBook ISBN: 979-8-8229-2162-7

SASYarts Studios USA

Saint Nicolas is a kind and loving spirit.
His brothers work through the year to bring joy to the world.
Santa Claus is here today to share a Christmas story.

1

*This is the story of Mama Ella Bear and her cub Little Paws.
He was almost one year old and it was Christmas Eve,
a very eventful night indeed!*

Santa's Workshop

LOADING DOCK

PAINTING   WRAPPING

ELF VILLAGE

LOADING DOCK

METAL
WORKSHOP
CARPENTRY

QUALITY CONTROL

SANTA'S HOUSE

SNOWBALL FIELD

DINING
HALL
KITCHEN
BAKERY
PANTRY

LOADING DOCK

SWEET SHOP

COURT YARD

REINDEER
PENS AND
SLEIGH
STORAGE

PENS AND
FEED
STORAGE

REINDEER
PENS

SCHOOL

LIBRARY

TRAIN OFFICE

POST OFFICE

NAUGHTY & NICE
COMPUTERS

LETTER STORAGE

GRAZING FIELD

ELF VILLAGE

ENTRY

TRAIN PLATFORM

REINDEER BARN

SWITCH TRACK

POLAR EXPRESS

I was grateful to everyone at North Pole City,
Mrs. Claus and the elves make a wonderful team.
Together we make Christmas magic around the world
for all the loving children.

But not everything was ready for the night's activities.
I heard Mrs. Claus gasp!
"We forgot to make Santa's cookies!"

I stepped into the bakery, what a sight to my eyes!
Elves were everywhere making my favorite cookies.
They even made spicy hot chocolate for my long winters ride.
I'm blessed to have such wonderful and thoughtful friends.

The gingerbread cookies looked adorable,
just like the elves that made them.
They were covered with icing with a sweet ginger surprise
that tasted scrumptious, delicious, the taste of heavenly delight.

We checked my list twice, and with all the work done,
I said " it's Jesus Christ's birthday so let's have some fun!"
Love and inspiration filled the air,
so much joy from a glorious affair!

Everyone from North Pole City was invited to the celebration.
My animal friends and all of my helpers will come.
We were excited for tomorrows big party because
who doesn't like to have fun?

Mama Ella bears giant claws are perfect for making snowballs.
She's our best worker and such a good mother.

Little Paws was happy helping his friends make
snowballs for the Christmas festivities.
When they were done, they were piled high as the trees,
a very impressive sight indeed.

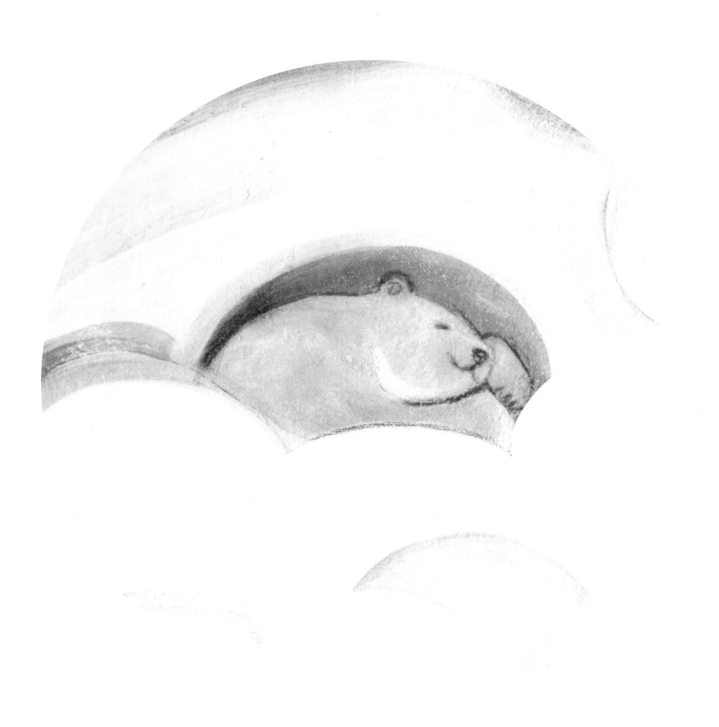

By 6 o'clock Little Paws was very tired.
His nose was frosty, his paws were sore; it was time for a nap.

Suddenly a very cold wind blew. WHOOSH!
A storm was approaching, snowmen were tripping and
branches were breaking. Mama Ella was frightened.
I heard her call out to Little Paws, "ROARRRRRR"
but he never answered.

I joined in the search for our friend, but it was getting very late.
It was difficult to see through the storm,
not even Rudolph's nose could light our way.
Yeti came to shield us from the freezing cold,
but still Little Paws was nowhere to be found.

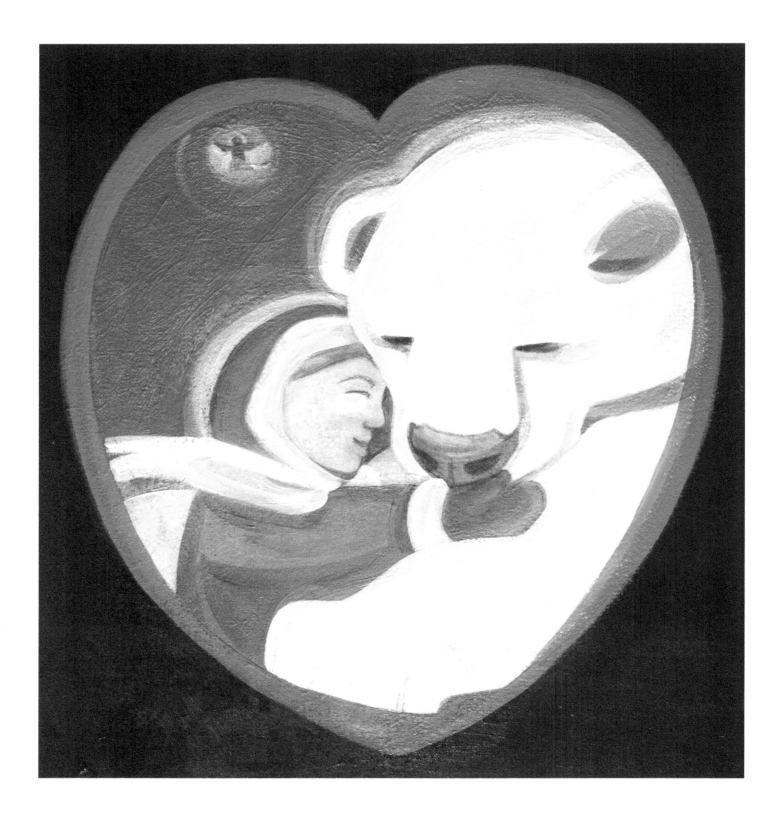

I wouldn't disappoint my children;
the sleigh ride around the world just couldn't wait.
I gathered the reindeer and loaded the gifts in my sleigh.
Before I took off I heard Mrs. Claus say a prayer with the bears.
" Jesus, please bring our families home safely. Amen."

The Christmas star was shining brightly when I returned home.
The children's presents were delivered.
I was broken hearted when I learned that
Little Paws was still missing.

Everyone gathered around and joined me in prayer to
St. Anthony the Saint of miracles and lost items.
We bowed our heads and said this prayer,
"Please St. Anthony help find Little Paws
and keep our hearts open. Amen."

What do you think happened next?

After the prayer was given, Little Paws
peeked out from behind a big bank of snow.
Rudolph greeted him with a lick on the nose and
Little Paws giggled from the tickle.

That clever little bear had dug a den deep in the snow
just like he was taught by Mama Ella.
The storm had raged through the night but
Little Paws was safe sleeping in his cozy den.

Mama Ella was so grateful her cub was safe.
She gave a big roar calling everyone to come and join
the North Pole celebration.
" ROARRRRRR!!"

The Snowball fight was so much fun,
it was the best day for everyone!

That very afternoon I created a toy for Little Paws
to remember his first Christmas. My gift to him
was wrapped with a big red bow and a tag that read:
"To a very special bear!"

Little Paws was so surprised when he opened his gift!
It was a teddy bear that looked just like him.
He gave me a big bear hug and then we walked outside
for all of North Pole City to hear the good news.

It's Christmas Day! God Bless you all.
Say a prayer for your family and friends.
Do your best to do things that are good, sharing
your love throughout the year.

Amen

Our protectors and saints mentioned in this story:

Jesus Christ
Born between 6 BC and 4 BC
Crucified April 3, he was 33 years old.
We celebrate Jesus Christ's birthday on December 25,
by giving gifts to people we love and others who need help.

St. Nicholas
March 15, 270 AD - December 6, 343 AD
With Santa's gift giving we feel the spirit of joy and charity.
Do not forget the real St. Nicholas who, like all saints points to Jesus.
That's the truest Christmas spirit of all.

St. Anthony of Padua
August 15, 1195 AD - June 13, 1231 AD
When any person prays to St Anthony with an open heart,
God always answers somehow.

Thanks to our amazing team that helped create this book.

SASYarts Studios USA
SASYarts.com

Story and illustrations by:
Sue Ann Alton Sanders
SASYarts.com

Photos and map design by:
Santa Paul H. Behrens, ORDM
SoYouPhotography.com